THE WORD OF WISDOM

DEVOTIONAL

Journal

A 31-Day Guide to Getting & Growing
In Wisdom from Proverbs

Janice Hylton Thompson

THE WORD OF WISDOM

DEVOTIONAL

Journal

Belongs To:

_____

_____

_____

www.janicehyltonblog.com

Would You Like a Surprise Freebie?

Snag it here @ www.janicehyltonblog.com

Instagram @ Author Janice Hylton

You can also email and say
Hey Janice @ janicehyltonblog@gmail.com

Be sure to subscribe to my Youtube Channels @

Study the Bible in One Year

Janice Hylton

Allegedly Janice

Show me Love On My Products @

1. Redbubble

2. Etsy

3. Tee Spring

@ Janice Hylton Tea Shop

King Solomon and the Two Mothers

One of my favorite bible stories of all times is King Solomon and the two mothers. I learned this story as a child in Sunday school. It began when two women who shared the same home had their babies three days apart.

Sadly, one of the mothers rolled over onto her baby during the night and smothered him to death. Then, shockingly, the dead baby's mother switched him with the live baby as the other mother slept. So, when the live baby's mother awoke, she found that her baby was dead.

However, as she examined the dead baby in the light, she realized that it was not hers. The live baby's mother claimed that the dead baby's mother had switched them during the night and had stolen her live baby. Well, both mothers went to King Solomon so that he could judge who the birth mother was.

Upon hearing the unfortunate events, King Solomon asked for a sword, and suggested splitting the baby in half and giving each mother half of the baby.

The live baby's mother screamed for King Solomon not to split the baby, but to give him to the other mother. Ironically, the other mother urged King Solomon to split the baby and give them each half.

Full of God's wisdom, King Solomon said not to kill the baby, but to give him to the mother who'd begged him not to kill the baby. Solomon knew that the real mother would rather let the other mother have her baby than see the baby killed and split in half.

And that my beloveth is wisdom.

Word of Wisdom
WOW

The book of Proverbs has always been a favorite of mine. Since my early teens, I have read a chapter of proverbs most days. Presently, in my mid-forties, I still read Proverbs to get a daily dose of wisdom. I can always find a gem that I call my word of wisdom for the day (my WOW!) I have too many favorite chapters and portions about wisdom to list here. However, the following are two of my favorites that tell us the reason for proverbs when talking about wisdom.

What is wisdom? A simple definition I learned as a teen is that wisdom knows what to do when you don't. Additionally, other definitions that I snagged from Google are that wisdom is the ability to discern or judge what is true, right, or lasting; insight. Wisdom is also common sense and good judgment. Finally, wisdom is the quality of having experience, knowledge, and good judgment; the quality of being wise.

Proverbs 1:1-9 [1] **The proverbs of Solomon the son of David, king of Israel;** [2] **To know wisdom and instruction; to perceive the words of understanding;** [3] **To receive the instruction of wisdom, justice, and judgment, and equity;** [4] **To give subtilty to the simple, to the young man knowledge and discretion.**

[5] **A wise man will hear, and will increase learning; and a man of understanding shall attain unto wise counsels:** [6] **To understand a proverb, and the interpretation; the words of the wise, and their dark sayings.** [7] **The fear of the Lord is the beginning of knowledge: but fools**

despise wisdom and instruction. [8] My son, hear the instruction of thy father, and forsake not the law of thy mother: [9] For they shall be an ornament of grace unto thy head, and chains about thy neck.

Why Wisdom?

King Solomon encouraged us to get wisdom. The word 'get' is a verb. A verb is an action word. So, you must put in some action to get wisdom. Word of Wisdom {WOW} will set you on the path of getting your daily dose of wisdom for every day. Begin your day every day by reading a chapter of Proverbs and writing down your WOW for each day.

Proverbs 4: 5-9 **5 Get wisdom, get understanding: forget it not; neither decline from the words of my mouth. 6 Forsake her not, and she shall preserve thee: love her, and she shall keep thee.**

7 Wisdom is the principal thing; therefore get wisdom: and with all thy getting get understanding.

8 Exalt her, and she shall promote thee: she shall bring thee to honor, when thou dost embrace her.

9 She shall give to thine head an ornament of grace: a crown of glory shall she deliver to thee.

Oh, I just love that portion right there!! What beautiful words from the wisest man that ever lived. As you search for your word of wisdom (WOW) each day, I pray that you will find them.

Write your WOW down, meditate on it, and apply it to your lives, situations, and circumstances. Remember that God, your father, is waiting for you to come to him and ask him for wisdom.

Proverbs 1

Date: _____

Which verse speaks to you? _____

Write verse _____: _____

_____

_____

Why does verse _____ speak to you? _____

_____

_____

_____

What does verse _____, mean to you? _____

_____

_____

_____

Was there a time you did not have the wisdom of verse _____? Why?

_____

_____

_____

How has verse _____, helped you to obtain wisdom? _____

_____

_____

In your own words, explain the verse _____. _____

_____

_____

_____

_____

WOW Thoughts & Notes

Date: _____

Proverbs 2

Date: ___

Which verse speaks to you? _____

Write verse _____ : _____

_____

_____

Why does verse _____ speak to you? _____

_____

_____

_____

What does verse _____, mean to you? _____

_____

_____

_____

Was there a time you did not have the wisdom of verse _____? Why?

_____

_____

_____

How has verse _____, helped you to obtain wisdom? _____

_____

_____

In your own words, explain the verse _____. _____

_____

_____

_____

_____

WOW Thoughts & Notes

Date: _____

_____
_____
_____
_____
_____
_____
_____
_____
_____
_____
_____
_____
_____
_____
_____
_____
_____
_____
_____
_____
_____
_____
_____
_____
_____
_____
_____

Proverbs 3

Date: _____

Which verse speaks to you? _____

Write verse _____: _____

_____

_____

Why does verse _____ speak to you? _____

_____

_____

_____

What does verse _____, mean to you? _____

_____

_____

_____

Was there a time you did not have the wisdom of verse _____? Why?

_____

_____

_____

How has verse _____, helped you to obtain wisdom? _____

_____

_____

In your own words, explain the verse _____. _____

_____

_____

_____

_____

WOW Thoughts & Notes   Date: _____

Proverbs 4

Date: ___

Which verse speaks to you? _____

Write verse _____ : _____

_____

_____

Why does verse _____ speak to you? _____

_____

_____

_____

What does verse _____, mean to you? _____

_____

_____

_____

Was there a time you did not have the wisdom of verse _____? Why?

_____

_____

_____

How has verse _____, helped you to obtain wisdom? _____

_____

_____

In your own words, explain the verse _____. _____

_____

_____

_____

_____

WOW Thoughts & Notes   Date: _____

_____
_____
_____
_____
_____
_____
_____
_____
_____
_____
_____
_____
_____
_____
_____
_____
_____
_____
_____
_____
_____
_____
_____
_____
_____
_____

Proverbs 5   Date: ____

Which verse speaks to you? _____

Write verse _____: _____

_____

_____

Why does verse _____ speak to you? _____

_____

_____

_____

What does verse _____, mean to you? _____

_____

_____

_____

Was there a time you did not have the wisdom of verse _____? Why?

_____

_____

_____

How has verse _____, helped you to obtain wisdom? _____

_____

_____

In your own words, explain the verse _____. _____

_____

_____

_____

_____

WOW Thoughts & Notes

Date: _____

Proverbs 6   Date: ___

Which verse speaks to you? _____

Write verse _____ : _____

_____

_____

Why does verse _____ speak to you? _____

_____

_____

_____

What does verse _____ , mean to you? _____

_____

_____

_____

Was there a time you did not have the wisdom of verse _____? Why?

_____

_____

_____

How has verse _____ , helped you to obtain wisdom? _____

_____

_____

In your own words, explain the verse _____ . _____

_____

_____

_____

_____

WOW Thoughts & Notes

Date: _____

_____
_____
_____
_____
_____
_____
_____
_____
_____
_____
_____
_____
_____
_____
_____
_____
_____
_____
_____
_____
_____
_____
_____
_____
_____
_____
_____
_____
_____

Proverbs 7

Date: _____

Which verse speaks to you? _____

Write verse _____: _____

_____

_____

Why does verse _____ speak to you? _____

_____

_____

_____

What does verse _____, mean to you? _____

_____

_____

_____

Was there a time you did not have the wisdom of verse _____? Why?

_____

_____

_____

How has verse _____, helped you to obtain wisdom? _____

_____

_____

In your own words, explain the verse _____. _____

_____

_____

_____

_____

WOW Thoughts & Notes

Date: _____

Proverbs 8   *Date:* ___

Which verse speaks to you? _____

Write verse _____ : _____

_____

_____

Why does verse _____ *speak to you?* _____

_____

_____

_____

What does verse _____ , *mean to you?* _____

_____

_____

_____

Was there a time you did not have the wisdom of verse _____ *? Why?*

_____

_____

_____

How has verse _____ , *helped you to obtain wisdom?* ____

_____

_____

In your own words, explain the verse _____ . _____

_____

_____

_____

_____

WOW Thoughts & Notes

Date: _____

Proverbs 9

Date: ___

Which verse speaks to you? _____

Write verse _____ : _____

_____

_____

Why does verse _____ speak to you? _____

_____

_____

_____

What does verse _____, mean to you? _____

_____

_____

_____

Was there a time you did not have the wisdom of verse _____? Why?

_____

_____

_____

How has verse _____, helped you to obtain wisdom? _____

_____

_____

In your own words, explain the verse _____. _____

_____

_____

_____

_____

WOW Thoughts & Notes

Date: _____

Proverbs 10

Date: __

Which verse speaks to you? _____

Write verse _____ : _____

_____

_____

Why does verse _____ speak to you? _____

_____

_____

_____

What does verse _____ , mean to you? _____

_____

_____

_____

Was there a time you did not have the wisdom of verse _____? Why?

_____

_____

_____

How has verse _____ , helped you to obtain wisdom? _____

_____

_____

In your own words, explain the verse _____ . _____

_____

_____

_____

_____

WOW Thoughts & Notes

Date: _____

Proverbs 11   Date: ___

Which verse speaks to you? _____

Write verse _____: _____

_____

_____

Why does verse _____ speak to you? _____

_____

_____

_____

What does verse _____, mean to you? _____

_____

_____

_____

Was there a time you did not have the wisdom of verse _____? Why?

_____

_____

_____

How has verse _____, helped you to obtain wisdom? _____

_____

_____

In your own words, explain the verse _____. _____

_____

_____

_____

_____

WOW Thoughts & Notes

Date: _____

Proverbs 12   *Date:* __

Which verse speaks to you? _____

Write verse _____ : _____

_____

_____

Why does verse _____ *speak to you?* _____

_____

_____

_____

What does verse _____ , *mean to you?* _____

_____

_____

_____

Was there a time you did not have the wisdom of verse _____ *? Why?*

_____

_____

_____

How has verse _____ , *helped you to obtain wisdom?* _____

_____

_____

In your own words, explain the verse _____ . _____

_____

_____

_____

_____

WOW Thoughts & Notes

Date: _____

Proverbs 13

Date: ___

Which verse speaks to you? _____

Write verse _____: _____

_____

_____

Why does verse _____ speak to you? _____

_____

_____

_____

What does verse _____, mean to you? _____

_____

_____

_____

Was there a time you did not have the wisdom of verse _____? Why?

_____

_____

_____

How has verse _____, helped you to obtain wisdom? _____

_____

_____

In your own words, explain the verse _____. _____

_____

_____

_____

_____

WOW Thoughts & Notes

Date: _____

Proverbs 14   Date: __

Which verse speaks to you? _____

Write verse _____ : _____

_____

_____

Why does verse _____ speak to you? _____

_____

_____

_____

What does verse _____, mean to you? _____

_____

_____

_____

Was there a time you did not have the wisdom of verse _____? Why?

_____

_____

_____

How has verse _____, helped you to obtain wisdom? _____

_____

_____

In your own words, explain the verse _____. _____

_____

_____

_____

_____

WOW Thoughts & Notes   Date: _____

_____
_____
_____
_____
_____
_____
_____
_____
_____
_____
_____
_____
_____
_____
_____
_____
_____
_____
_____
_____
_____
_____
_____
_____
_____
_____

Proverbs 15

Date: ___

Which verse speaks to you? _____

Write verse _____: _____

_____

_____

Why does verse _____ speak to you? _____

_____

_____

_____

What does verse _____, mean to you? _____

_____

_____

_____

Was there a time you did not have the wisdom of verse _____? Why?

_____

_____

_____

How has verse _____, helped you to obtain wisdom? _____

_____

_____

In your own words, explain the verse _____. _____

_____

_____

_____

_____

WOW Thoughts & Notes

Date: _____

Proverbs 16

Which verse speaks to you? _____

Write verse _____ : _____

_____

_____

Why does verse _____ speak to you? _____

_____

_____

_____

What does verse _____, mean to you? _____

_____

_____

_____

Was there a time you did not have the wisdom of verse _____? Why?

_____

_____

_____

How has verse _____, helped you to obtain wisdom? _____

_____

_____

In your own words, explain the verse _____. _____

_____

_____

_____

_____

WOW Thoughts & Notes

Date: _____

Proverbs 17   *Date:* __

Which verse speaks to you? _____

Write verse _____: _____

_____

_____

Why does verse _____ *speak to you?* _____

_____

_____

_____

What does verse _____, *mean to you?* _____

_____

_____

_____

Was there a time you did not have the wisdom of verse _____*? Why?*

_____

_____

_____

How has verse _____, *helped you to obtain wisdom?* _____

_____

_____

In your own words, explain the verse _____. _____

_____

_____

_____

_____

WOW Thoughts & Notes   Date: _____

Proverbs 18   Date: __

Which verse speaks to you? _____

Write verse _____ : _____

_____

_____

Why does verse _____ speak to you? _____

_____

_____

_____

What does verse _____, mean to you? _____

_____

_____

_____

Was there a time you did not have the wisdom of verse _____? Why?

_____

_____

_____

How has verse _____, helped you to obtain wisdom? _____

_____

_____

In your own words, explain the verse _____. _____

_____

_____

_____

_____

WOW Thoughts & Notes

Date: _____

Proverbs 19

Date: ___

Which verse speaks to you? _____

Write verse _____ : _____

_____

_____

Why does verse _____ speak to you? _____

_____

_____

_____

What does verse _____, mean to you? _____

_____

_____

_____

Was there a time you did not have the wisdom of verse _____? Why?

_____

_____

_____

How has verse _____, helped you to obtain wisdom? _____

_____

_____

In your own words, explain the verse _____. _____

_____

_____

_____

_____

WOW Thoughts & Notes

Date: _____

Proverbs 20

Date: __

Which verse speaks to you? _____

Write verse _____ : _____

_____

_____

Why does verse _____ speak to you? _____

_____

_____

_____

What does verse _____, mean to you? _____

_____

_____

_____

Was there a time you did not have the wisdom of verse _____? Why?

_____

_____

_____

How has verse _____, helped you to obtain wisdom? _____

_____

_____

In your own words, explain the verse _____. _____

_____

_____

_____

_____

WOW Thoughts & Notes   Date: _____

Proverbs 21   Date: ___

Which verse speaks to you? _____

Write verse _____ : _____

_____

_____

Why does verse _____ speak to you? _____

_____

_____

_____

What does verse _____, mean to you? _____

_____

_____

_____

Was there a time you did not have the wisdom of verse _____? Why?

_____

_____

_____

How has verse _____, helped you to obtain wisdom? _____

_____

_____

In your own words, explain the verse _____. _____

_____

_____

_____

_____

WOW Thoughts & Notes

Date: _____

Proverbs 22

Date: __

Which verse speaks to you? _____

Write verse _____: _____

_____

_____

Why does verse _____ speak to you? _____

_____

_____

_____

What does verse _____, mean to you? _____

_____

_____

_____

Was there a time you did not have the wisdom of verse _____? Why?

_____

_____

_____

How has verse _____, helped you to obtain wisdom? _____

_____

_____

In your own words, explain the verse _____. _____

_____

_____

_____

_____

WOW Thoughts & Notes

Date: _____

Proverbs 23

Date: ___

Which verse speaks to you? _____

Write verse _____ : _____

_____

_____

Why does verse _____ speak to you? _____

_____

_____

_____

What does verse _____ , mean to you? _____

_____

_____

_____

Was there a time you did not have the wisdom of verse _____ ? Why?

_____

_____

_____

How has verse _____ , helped you to obtain wisdom? _____

_____

_____

In your own words, explain the verse _____ . _____

_____

_____

_____

_____

WOW Thoughts & Notes

Date: _____

Proverbs 24

Date: __

Which verse speaks to you? _____

Write verse _____ : _____

_____

_____

Why does verse _____ speak to you? _____

_____

_____

_____

What does verse _____, mean to you? _____

_____

_____

_____

Was there a time you did not have the wisdom of verse _____? Why?

_____

_____

_____

How has verse _____, helped you to obtain wisdom? _____

_____

_____

In your own words, explain the verse _____. _____

_____

_____

_____

_____

WOW Thoughts & Notes

Date: _____

Proverbs 25

Date: ___

Which verse speaks to you? _____

Write verse _____ : _____

_____

_____

Why does verse _____ speak to you? _____

_____

_____

_____

What does verse _____ , mean to you? _____

_____

_____

_____

Was there a time you did not have the wisdom of verse _____ ? Why?

_____

_____

_____

How has verse _____ , helped you to obtain wisdom? _____

_____

_____

In your own words, explain the verse _____ . _____

_____

_____

_____

_____

WOW Thoughts & Notes

Date: _____

Proverbs 26   *Date:* __

Which verse speaks to you? _____

Write verse _____ : _____
_____
_____

Why does verse _____ *speak to you?* _____
_____
_____
_____

What does verse _____ , *mean to you?* _____
_____
_____
_____

Was there a time you did not have the wisdom of verse _____? *Why?*
_____
_____
_____

How has verse _____ , *helped you to obtain wisdom?* _____
_____
_____

In your own words, explain the verse _____ . _____
_____
_____
_____
_____

WOW Thoughts & Notes

Date: _____

Proverbs 27   *Date:* __

Which verse speaks to you? _____

Write verse _____ : _____

_____

_____

Why does verse _____ *speak to you?* _____

_____

_____

_____

What does verse _____ , *mean to you?* _____

_____

_____

_____

Was there a time you did not have the wisdom of verse _____ *? Why?*

_____

_____

_____

How has verse _____ , *helped you to obtain wisdom?* _____

_____

_____

In your own words, explain the verse _____ . _____

_____

_____

_____

_____

WOW Thoughts & Notes

Date: _____

Proverbs 28   *Date:* __

Which verse speaks to you? _____

Write verse _____ : _____

_____

_____

Why does verse _____ *speak to you?* _____

_____

_____

_____

What does verse _____ , *mean to you?* _____

_____

_____

_____

Was there a time you did not have the wisdom of verse _____? *Why?*

_____

_____

_____

How has verse _____ , *helped you to obtain wisdom?* _____

_____

_____

In your own words, explain the verse _____ . _____

_____

_____

_____

_____

WOW Thoughts & Notes

Date: _____

Proverbs 29   Date: __

Which verse speaks to you? _____

Write verse _____ : _____

_____

_____

Why does verse _____ speak to you? _____

_____

_____

_____

What does verse _____ , mean to you? _____

_____

_____

_____

Was there a time you did not have the wisdom of verse _____? Why?

_____

_____

_____

How has verse _____ , helped you to obtain wisdom? _____

_____

_____

In your own words, explain the verse _____ . _____

_____

_____

_____

_____

WOW Thoughts & Notes

Date: _____

Proverbs 30   *Date:* __

Which verse speaks to you? _____

Write verse _____ : _____

_____

_____

Why does verse _____ *speak to you?* _____

_____

_____

_____

What does verse _____ , *mean to you?* _____

_____

_____

_____

Was there a time you did not have the wisdom of verse _____? *Why?*

_____

_____

_____

How has verse _____ , *helped you to obtain wisdom?* _____

_____

_____

In your own words, explain the verse _____ . _____

_____

_____

_____

_____

WOW Thoughts & Notes

Date: _____

Proverbs 31   *Date:* __

Which verse speaks to you? _____

Write verse _____ : _____

_____

_____

Why does verse _____ *speak to you?* _____

_____

_____

_____

What does verse _____ , *mean to you?* _____

_____

_____

_____

Was there a time you did not have the wisdom of verse _____ *? Why?*

_____

_____

_____

How has verse _____ , *helped you to obtain wisdom?* _____

_____

_____

In your own words, explain the verse _____ . _____

_____

_____

_____

_____

WOW Thoughts & Notes

Date: _____

WOW Thoughts & Notes

Date: _____

WOW Thoughts & Notes

Date: _____

WOW Thoughts & Notes

Date: _____

WOW Thoughts & Notes

Date: _____

WOW Thoughts & Notes

Date: _____

WOW Thoughts & Notes

Date: _____

WOW Thoughts & Notes

Date: _____

WOW Thoughts & Notes

Date: _____

About the Author

Janice is a wife to her wonderful husband, Michael Sr., and mom of two children born 20 years apart: Janice's beautiful and fashionable daughter, Alexia, and her inquisitive and joyful son, Michael Jr.

Janice loves to read and write. She writes passionately about subjects that mean the most to her. Additionally, Janice loves to tackle those "rock the boat" subjects. Janice loves to spend time with her family, making their favorite meals, watching movies, enjoying a day at the park, shopping, doing girly stuff with Alexia, and playing and learning with her son Michael Jr.

Janice is the author of several books and has been writing for over 20 years. Her published books include:

1. **Praying for Our Children**
2. **In Christ I Am**
3. **In Christ, I Am Prayer Journal**
4. **In Christ, I Am Bible Study Journal**
5. **Moments of Gratitude**
6. **The Phenomenon of Donald J Trump The GOP Nominee**
7. **The Naked Wife**
8. **23 Types of Guys You Might Meet**
9. **31 Days to NOT Being A Girlfriend If You Want to Be a Wife**
10. **How to Not Give Boyfriends Husband Benefits**
11. **10 Years a Girlfriend**

Additionally, Janice blogs @ www.janicehyltonblog.com

Connect with Janice on:

Instagram @ Author Janice Hylton

Facebook: Janice Hylton Blog and Author Janice Hylton

You can also connect with Janice on YouTube @

1. Janice Hylton
2. Study the Bible in One Year
3. Allegedly Janice